STARLESS MIDNIGHT

Laura Shenton

STARLESS MIDNIGHT

Laura Shenton

Iridescent Toad Publishing

Iridescent Toad Publishing.

Cover by RJ Creatives.

First edition. ISBN: 978-1-8380186-2-7

Prologue

Evelyn walked with a lightness in her step, relishing the coolness of the forest air on her skin. She could hear birds chirping in the distance and the rustling of leaves in the gentle breeze. The sunlight filtered in through the trees, dappling the ground with a golden glow.

She took a deep breath, inhaling the fresh scent of pine and wildflowers. She loved the peacefulness of nature, and the way it made her feel calm and grounded. It was a welcome change from the chaos of the town, where she constantly had to be on her guard to protect her true identity as a witch. Although she had managed to do it every day for each of her twenty-three years, it was always at the front of her mind. Only behind closed doors in the presence of family could witches be truly at ease.

As she walked deeper into the forest, Evelyn came across a clearing. The grass was soft and lush, and the sun shone down on it with a radiant intensity. She paused for a moment, taking in the beauty of the scene before her. She felt a sense of serenity wash over her, as though the forest itself was cradling her in its calm embrace.

Her peaceful reverie was interrupted by a sound – one that refocused her attention back to the present moment and pulled on her heartstrings. Somewhere nearby, a child was crying.

Evelyn followed the sound. It took her to the sorry sight of a little girl sitting on the ground, tears streaming down her face. She had fallen and cut her knee. Deep crimson blood seeped from the wound, the rivulets running down her small, pale shin.

For her own safety, Evelyn had always kept to herself and was reluctant to get involved. It was a habit she had grown used to as a witch in a town full of normals. On this occasion though, although she hesitated at first, something inside her couldn't bear to see the young girl looking so distressed.

She approached the girl and crouched down beside her.

"Are you ok?" she asked gently.

The girl looked up at her, her cheeks glistening with shed tears.

"I fell," she said, her voice trembling. "And there's a stone stuck in my knee. It hurts so much."

Evelyn could see the small stone. Gleaming like a miniature bead of aquamarine, it was embedded in the girl's knee – and at an awkward angle too. Although the wound was tiny, it looked incredibly sore. Even the smallest of movements would surely send a sharp jolt of shock through every nearby nerve. Not only did the stone need to be removed as a matter of urgency, but Evelyn knew that if the wound itself was left untreated, it could become infected and cause serious harm.

Evelyn gently touched the girl's knee, causing her to wince in pain.

"It's ok, I'm not going to hurt you," she said

softly, offering a reassuring smile.

"My mummy and daddy told me not to come to the forest," she whimpered. "I know I should have listened to them. They're going to be so angry with me."

Evelyn knew what it was like to be afraid of authority figures. Sensing the fear in the girl's voice, she knew the pain in her knee was only part of her distress. She couldn't bear to think of the girl having to face the wrath of her strict parents.

It moved Evelyn to see the girl so upset. She wanted to help her, to take away her pain and make everything better. But at the same time, she knew that using her magic could put her in grave danger. In the town, witches were feared and hunted; the consequences of being discovered could be deadly.

She sighed heavily, feeling the weight of her conflicting emotions. She closed her eyes, trying to gather her thoughts. Her mind raced with the reasons as to why she shouldn't use her magic, but faced with a nasty wound on an innocent and scared child all alone in the forest, her doubts melted away. She made the decision to use her magic to help the girl, come what may. It was a risk, but one that she felt she had to take.

"Let me help you," Evelyn said softly. "I'll make sure there's no sign of your injury, and your parents won't know that you were hurt."

The girl sniffled and watched in wonder as Evelyn set to work.

Placing her hand on the girl's knee, Evelyn closed her eyes in concentration. She visualised the small stone embedded in the torn flesh, and focused her magic on it.

With a sudden burst of energy, a warm light emanated from Evelyn's hand and enveloped the area around the girl's knee. The girl gasped in surprise as she felt a sudden release of pressure.

Evelyn opened her eyes to see the small stone dislodged from the wound. As she closed her eyes again and continued to concentrate, the light coming from her hand began to transform into a soft, green glow. The girl gasped in awe as Evelyn's magic knitted the wound back together, erasing any trace of the injury.

Finally, the glow faded away, and Evelyn opened her eyes. The girl looked down at her knee in amazement. It was completely healed.

Evelyn breathed a sigh of relief, grateful that her magic had worked without drawing any unwanted attention. She knew she couldn't let her guard down, but for now, she was happy that she'd been able to help.

"It doesn't hurt anymore!" the girl exclaimed, her face lighting up in relief. "Thank you so much! How did you do that?"

Evelyn smiled at the girl; her innocence was endearing.

"I have a special power that can heal people," she explained. "But you have to promise not to tell anyone, ok?"

The girl nodded eagerly.

"I won't tell anyone," she said. "I promise!"

"Good," Evelyn said as she stood up to dust her clothes down. "Now, you'd better hurry back to your parents. They'll be worried about you."

"Thank you," the girl said, looking up at Evelyn with big, bright eyes.

"You're welcome. Now run along, and be careful next time."

Evelyn watched as the girl ran off towards home, her heart light and her step quick. She knew she had taken a huge risk, and that the consequences of her actions could be severe. Despite this, she was convinced that she'd done the right thing, and that her magic had been used for good. The internal conflict within her raged on, but for now, she felt a sense of peace knowing that the young girl was ok.

14

Chapter One

Evelyn gasped for air as she sprinted away, her pursuers hot on her heels. The night sky was illuminated by a menacing blaze of torches as the mob brandished their weapons like an army of demons. They were an unstoppable force of rage, the cacophony of their cries filling the air. Evelyn could almost taste their fierce desire to hunt her down. Their relentless determination filled her with terror.

She had to find a safe spot – and quickly. Her dark hair whipped in the wind as her feet flew over the rugged terrain. Her lightweight, airy garments, dyed in rich hues, waved and fluttered with every gust.

Her breathing was ragged as she ran, her strength the only thing keeping her going. She was thankful for her peak condition, having honed her hunting skills since childhood. Now those same skills were proving to be useful as she found herself being chased, becoming the hunted rather than the hunter.

The howling of the hounds drove her onwards, making her shudder with dread. The starlight glinted off of her sapphire eyes, but not quite brightly enough to give her away.

She had no choice but to flee her hometown, her identity as a witch no longer concealed. It had cost her parents their lives. She tried hard to push the images that reminded her of them away from the forefront of her thoughts; survival was the only goal right now. It had to be.

Trees whirred past, their sharp needles reminding her of the mob's weapons. She assumed the pitchforks were meant to rip her open, but she would not let them succeed; she'd survive somehow, no matter what she had to do.

The distant barking and shouting became quieter as she ran further into the forest.

Despite her terror, she had to focus on finding somewhere secure to hide. A cave was not an option; the dogs would follow her in, and then she'd be trapped.

Although time wasn't on her side, she couldn't afford to make the wrong decision. Her stomach churned with dread, intensifying the sinking feeling inside her. The angry voices of the crowd were drawing closer and more menacing. Her hair fell in front of her face as she searched desperately for somewhere to hide.

Thankfully, she spotted the sight of water in the distance. Charging towards the reflection of the moon on the nearby lake, she couldn't help but feel grateful for its presence. Without hesitation, she took a leap into the cold water below, instantly soaking her clothes. The icy temperature made her shiver as it enveloped her entire body. But still, she knew that being in the water would give her an advantage over the normals – they were even less able to cope with such conditions.

Her swimming was powerful enough to keep her afloat despite the additional weight of her clothing. Her muscles moved rhythmically as she pushed through the water. She knew that eventually, her pursuers could gain on her via a different route, and that any head start she had gained wouldn't last forever.

Swimming vigorously, as she arrived at the other side of the lake, she inadvertently swallowed several gulps of water. After pulling herself up onto level ground and coughing up the unpleasantly murky liquid, she pushed her palms against her forehead to suppress the dizziness that threatened to overwhelm her. Despite her discomfort, she was certain that she had made the right choice. Not only would the mob be deterred by the water, but through having been in it herself, she had hopefully managed to obscure her scent from the hounds, if only a little.

Still though, if the mob were determined enough, they would find another route. She doubted very much that they would relent. For years, they had aspired to eradicate her kind. She shuddered with blind rage as she thought back to the injustice of it all.

Sprinting once more, she reached out and grabbed some petals as the trees and wildflowers blurred past her. She rubbed them into her skin and clothing, hoping to further mask her scent from the hounds. She was light-footed enough that in the dark, it would be hard for anyone to spot her tracks. At least until daybreak, having gained ground, she had the vital scope to remain invisible from detection.

Flexing her arms and legs, she climbed up the branches of a large tree, using her upper body strength to pull herself higher and higher. When she reached the thickest, widest part of the tree, she paused. All that could be heard was the still of the night. A cold breeze blew across her face, reminding her that winter was on its way and that soon, should she survive the mob, without a place to call home, she would be left exposed to the harsh elements.

The minor scratches she'd obtained from moving into the tree were insignificant compared to the more serious injuries she'd sustained when the angry mob had first attacked her home. The smell of smoke still lingered in her nose, and the intense pain – both physical and emotional – caused her to burst into tears.

Frantically, she undid some of the fastenings on her clothing, and began to tear off strips of fabric to serve as makeshift bandages. As she did so, she inspected her injuries. Her body was covered in deep, red welts. Her skin was charred from when her home had been set alight, and she had countless throbbing bruises from the mob's strikes where they had landed multiple blows against her. However, her body told only a fraction of the story that caused her the greatest distress: she had lost everything.

Using her arm to dab away the tears from her eyes, she stifled a sob as she pressed tattered pieces of her clothing onto the cuts that were still bleeding. Not only did she want to serve her wounds, but she had to do everything possible to keep her scent away from the mob's insatiable hounds.

Leaning back against the sturdy tree trunk, Evelyn shivered, and shut her eyes, wishing she could rest just for a moment before running again. Although she had a track record of being a successful hunter, surviving this chase was far more challenging.

Despite her laboured protests, she couldn't

fight the weariness that threatened to consume her. Darkness engulfed the crevices of her mind as her dreams arrived to replay the events that had caused her to lose everything.

It was all so sudden and relentless. A blinding burst of light ignited everything in sight. Having lived in fear for so long that something like this could happen, Evelyn's father knew his fate was sealed. However, he was determined to protect his daughter at all costs.

Evelyn pleaded with him to let her stay. She wanted to negotiate with the hostile crowd. Even though she was willing to fight as a last resort, her parents insisted on taking the brunt of the mob's violence. They wanted her to have every possible chance of escape.

Her parents screamed at her to flee without looking back, but she disregarded their warning. As soon as she'd crawled out of the house through a shattered window, her skin torn from the broken glass, she looked back to witness a scene of gruesome terror.

Her father had been skewered by multiple

pitchforks; some of them were buried into his flesh close to the hilt. As the tips of the hatred-fuelled weapons were shoved deeper into his body, blood dribbled abundantly from his vast array of wounds. It stained his torn clothes and pooled in a river of crimson around his feet, and the ground beneath him – upon which he could barely still stand.

As the stench of blood – a pungent blend of iron and copper – hung in the air, his eyes bulged from his head as he glared helplessly at his daughter with his last thoughts. His face twisted in agony, and as his body shook and convulsed violently, he endured a long, drawn-out demise, writhing in pain until his last breath.

"DEATH TO THE WITCH!" chanted the bloodcurdling chorus of the frenzied crowd.

Men, women, and even some older children, were screaming and shouting at the top of their lungs in a flurry of mass hysteria. The air was thick with rage and hatred. Their cries reverberated against the remaining walls of the burning house, and out into the streets.

The mob was growing more maniacal by the

second, driven by the promise of retribution and justice against the family they believed were a curse on their town. The strength of their conviction growing with each passing moment, their faces twisted with anger and contorted with the fervour of their chant as they surged forward with determination, not an ounce of apology in their conduct.

Outnumbered and unable to defend herself against the onslaught from the raging mob, Evelyn's mother was restrained with pieces of twine and bound to a heavy oak chair. With no regard for her impending suffering, the mob set her ablaze with their torches.

The smell of burning flesh wafted through the air, accompanied by the tortured shrieks of the poor woman. The sound of the crackling flames only added to the cacophony of horror that assailed Evelyn's senses. She could only watch in stunned disbelief as her beloved mother was taken by the flames. She felt powerless, unable to do anything but stand in terror-stricken silence as her sweet mother's body was gradually reduced to ashes.

Despite every fibre of her being screaming at her to run away from the nightmare unfolding *before her, Evelyn remained rooted to the spot, frozen with fear at what had befallen her once-tranquil and comforting family home.*

Amidst the pandemonium, some of the angry crowd also perished. Some were killed by their neighbour's pitchforks, whilst others were trampled underfoot in the chaos. Flailing bodies and screams filled the air. Although most of the aggressors managed to flee unscathed, like an infestation of cockroaches, numerous and resilient, for every one who met their end, several more eagerly stepped up to fill the void.

A wave of nausea washed over Evelyn, causing her abdominal muscles to ache and clench. She doubled over and expelled the contents of her stomach onto the cobblestones. Her throat burned and her vision blurred as tears streamed down her cheeks. Waves of sorrow and rage drowned her as she choked and sobbed uncontrollably. She felt broken beyond repair.

After a few moments, she managed to compose herself just enough to begin thinking ahead. The cruel reality sank in that she was now completely alone and unprotected.

Despite still feeling sick and dizzy, she knew that the menacing stares from the mob meant only one thing: she was their next target.

The mob stood facing her with pitchforks in hand, ready to pounce on their next victim. A terrifying sense of finality began to seep in through every pore, keeping Evelyn paralysed to the spot. She knew that if she was to have any chance of escape, she would need to run, but still she couldn't move. Desperate to escape and charge off into the night, she even prayed that something, anything, would grant her the grace of being able to leave behind the sorrow and terror that threatened to end her, but still she couldn't move...

Startled, Evelyn awoke with a jolt, shaking her head and brushing aside the tangled locks of hair that had fallen across her face. Gasping for air, she gazed up at the sky, which remained shrouded in darkness. Uncertain of how much time had elapsed since she had drifted off, she concluded that it couldn't have been much. After a moment, she began to knead her temples, exhaling deeply in an attempt to calm herself.

She was relieved to observe that her bleeding

had finally ceased. Desperate for respite, she winced at the deep-seated discomfort that permeated her entire body. In addition to the wounds, the sprint had left her feeling significantly drained. After taking a vigilant look around at the surrounding area, she wearily scaled her way down the tree. When she reached the base of it, she rubbed her eyes, determined to focus and formulate a strategy. If necessary, she could gather some berries to sustain herself, if only for a short period.

Is this because I helped that poor girl in the forest that day?

Evelyn could have kicked herself for having been so naive. She'd let her emotions get the better of her. Although the little girl wouldn't have wished her any harm, it was plausible that she lacked the maturity to maintain the silence she had promised.

Maybe it wasn't the little girl. Maybe mine and my parents' identity was discovered another way.

Even in the dire circumstances, Evelyn didn't want to wrongly accuse anyone of having caused her so much trouble. She didn't want to hold a grudge against anyone – least of all those who didn't deserve it. Besides, rumours were always being passed around as part of the standard paranoid gossip amongst some of the more outspoken townsfolk.

Before Evelyn could finish her thoughts, a snarl from the nearby bushes interrupted her. When she spun around swiftly, she found herself facing a hound, its tanned fur bristling in the darkness. It snarled again, deeper this time, its lips curling back to reveal sharp ivory teeth. Its malevolent onyx eyes glowed with a thirst for her blood. They seemed to bore into her very soul as the hound prepared to stalk closer, the dust on the ground unsettling beneath its paws.

Evelyn's scream pierced the air. Her heart pounding in her chest, she sprinted away.

With the townsfolk dedicated in their need to cause her harm, she ran into the shadows of the forest ahead. Despite her emotions being in turmoil, fear gripped her the most. She knew she needed to be brave and not let her parents' sacrifice be in vain.

The cacophony of maniacal voices echoed behind her, ringing in her ears.

"Kill the witch! Kill her!"

Chapter Two

Haunting recollections of her nightmarish ordeal flooded Evelyn's thoughts, turning her initial tendrils of fear into a potent surge of rage. Nevertheless, she recognised that making a hasty decision could lead to dire consequences. It was crucial for her to maintain composure, keep her wits about her, and continue fleeing.

Although she continued to cover ground, after a while, she had to reduce her pace and lean against a tree to catch her breath, her chest heaving with exhaustion. Though she had managed to temporarily outrun the mob and their dogs, she realised that her energy reserves were dwindling.

In an attempt to staunch the scent of her sweat, she once again began to smear mud and nearby herbs all over herself. She hoped the aromas would be sufficient to mask her presence and elude the hounds. She was convinced she could still hear their baying, along with the humans' hateful chorus. The sounds seemed faint, and as though several groups had split up into teams and moved in different directions to scour the area for her.

Suddenly, a rabid hound came from nowhere, and before Evelyn had time to register what was happening, it had latched its jaws around her forearm.

She screamed in anguish. The sensation was uniquely excruciating, like nothing she had ever felt before. No witch had ever been able to heal their own wounds. By all accounts, they were mortal and could only use their magic to aid the healing of others. Never before had Evelyn wished so badly that just once, she could self-heal.

She shrieked in agony as three sharp pikes from the tip of a pitchfork slammed into her shoulder. Straight away, her gaze met the eyes of the man responsible. He seemed devoid of any shred of humanity or rationality as his lips twisted into a wicked smile.

"I've got you now," he said with venom. "Your death will be slow and torturous; I'll make sure of that. I've never done anything like this before, but I'm going to enjoy it."

The man's words and overall demeanour made Evelyn's skin crawl. The hair on the back of her neck stood on end as she grasped the situation. With no choice but to draw on her magic as a last resort, she honed in on the strands coursing through her veins. In a whispered incantation, she wove a spell of gentle persuasion, imploring the hound to release its grip on her. As the enchantment unfolded, the once-rabid gleam in the hound's eyes softened as the creature succumbed to a subtle feeling of tranquillity.

Caught between the instinct to obey its master and the soothing influence of the hypnotic enchantment, the hound hesitated. Slowly though, its jaws loosened their grip, and Evelyn withdrew her arm, grateful for the subtle dance of magic that had diffused the threat without harm. It wasn't the hound's fault that its owner was cruel.

Confused by the unfamiliarity of sensations it had just experienced, the dog scurried away from Evelyn and then further away from its master. With its tail tucked between its legs, it whined softly as it trotted off into the distance.

Evelyn then redirected her attention to the man, a faint smile passing across her face as she wrapped her fingers around the handle of the pitchfork lodged in her shoulder. Grimacing at the tendrils of pain it caused with its movement, she yanked it out, letting her blood trickle freely from the wound. A snarl escaped her lips as her eyes locked onto the man's confused stare.

"I've been misjudged," she said coldly.

Her knuckles white as she clenched the pitchfork with sheer disgust, in one violent motion, she furiously hurled it away.

His expression one of pure hatred and malice, the man charged towards Evelyn. In panic, she raised her hands, and with a burst of magic, he was slammed to the cold, hard ground like a ragdoll. Shocked and winded from the force, he couldn't move.

With a flick of her wrist, Evelyn surrounded

herself in a golden glow of magic. Her features contorted and twisted as she advanced forward and proceeded to pin the man down, his body writhing in a hopeless blend of bewilderment and defiance. The otherworldly glow that surrounded her body only grew brighter as she maintained her grip on the man. She glared into his eyes and saw the absolute terror that had overtaken him.

"Get out of my sight," she said firmly. "I mean you no harm, but I will not hesitate to defend myself."

For a moment, the man thought he might die. He looked truly defeated and prepared to meet his creator as he blurted out a nonsensical stream of words that Evelyn could only decipher as last-resort begging. True to her word though, she showed mercy and released him from her grip. The man lay there, gasping for breath, his body battered and bruised. He looked up at the witch, alarm and anger still etched on his face.

"Go," Evelyn commanded. "Leave this place, and never return."

The man stumbled to his feet. His legs were

shaking beneath him and his face was ghostly pale. He glanced at Evelyn one last time before turning and running away into the distance.

Evelyn watched him go, her heart pounding in her chest. She had never used her magic like that before, and the experience had left her shaken. As her frenzy began to subside, she was hit with a horrible pang of guilt, but she knew that in that moment, she had done what she'd needed to do in order to protect herself.

Never have I used my powers for anything other than good. How has it come to this?!

The sound of approaching people spurred her into action; she had to get away, and fast.

She ran with conviction, the wind roaring fiercely in her ears as she searched for shelter. Finally, after some time, she stumbled upon a tiny alcove just big enough to fit her body. The entrance was obscured by an overgrown bush that she had to push aside, wincing as the thorns pricked her skin.

Curled up in silence with only the bush to

hide behind, Evelyn drew in a sharp breath when the sound of footsteps closed in. A single tear rolled down her face as she heard the hounds sniffing, indicating that they had tracked her down. To her surprise, however, the dogs yelped and scurried away. The hunters shouted out in confusion, but the dogs refused to lead their masters to their target. They sensed an unfamiliar aura, something to be left alone.

Evelyn heard the sound of heavy footsteps coming nearer and nearer until they stopped right in front of her. She held her breath and tightly shut her eyes as a gruff voice echoed around her.

"You lost her scent?! Don't be ridiculous!" one of the men declared.

"She must have gone in a different direction," another man said. "The hounds aren't giving us any indication of the witch's whereabouts around here."

"Can you hear that?" the first man said in an angry growl. "What are they yelling about over there?"

Eventually, the two men left, and Evelyn breathed a sigh of relief. Maybe it was the remnants of her sudden surge of power that had driven the hounds away – just like when she had spooked that hound and its master. Whatever the reason, she felt thankful as she waited for the sound of footsteps to fade completely.

Exhausted, with her adrenaline rapidly dissipating, Evelyn noticed that her skin was coated with smears of blood that were beginning to harden and dry. As the first rays of morning sunshine began to illuminate the horizon, a chill ran through her body. Squinting out from behind the bush at the landscape ahead of her, she sensed that sleep was a risk she couldn't afford to take.

Despite her efforts to stay awake, it was no use; she soon drifted off to sleep. The brief slumber she had managed to catch while in the tree had been insufficient. Having resisted the overwhelming fatigue for as long as possible, it had now caught up with her. Tormented by horrific dreams and waking multiple times during the day with a gasp, she managed to keep resting until dusk.

***

The stars glittered in the night sky as a bitter chill swept through the air. Evelyn shivered, dreading the upcoming winter that would bring no respite. With nowhere to go, and with no food, she had no clue what her future would entail. She brought her hands to her face and wept softly, unable to stop the tears. The harsh reality was too much for her – each time it struck, it hurt more than the last.

Mustering her courage, she focused her gaze on the space outside the small alcove. Confident that her skin would heal eventually, she gathered up the determination to push through the thorny branches again. Although the need to stay safe could not be ignored, she couldn't deny the rumble of hunger that growled in her stomach.

Every rustle of leaves, every snap of a twig beneath her feet, sent a jolt through Evelyn's nerves as she navigated the dense forest. The shadows seemed to whisper ominous secrets, and the wind carried echoes of imagined footsteps. She moved with the cautious precision of a small prey animal being stalked. The silence was both her ally and her adversary. Each hushed moment carried the potential for a sudden eruption of hostility. Anxiety had seized her body, keeping her muscles tight and making it hard to shake off the churning dread in her gut.

Mercifully, although the bright moonlight gave her some measure of comfort, the clouds gathering in the sky warned her that she should hurry and find shelter soon. As she stepped out of the forest, the grass tickled her already-battered legs, her ragged clothing barely covering them. She paused briefly to catch her breath, and then continued her journey across the open expanse.

Hours later, Evelyn found herself in a different, unfamiliar forest. Although she was relieved to have left what was once her hometown far behind, she was acutely aware that she was no closer to having any new comforts. And so, she began to scavenge for food, reaching deep into the bushes and picking off any edible plants and scarce berries that had managed to survive the looming frigidity of the season.

Eventually, she also managed to gather enough wood to kindle a fire. The comfort of its heat would be welcome in the cold night.

Oddly, the animals of the forest didn't seem interested in her presence. As she ate some of the plants she'd gathered, she tried to ignore the animals and their sweet nature, for she would soon need to set some traps that would help her catch some meat – a vital source of protein in the circumstances.

With no sturdy roof overhead, she sought refuge amidst the trees, her only companions the rustling leaves and the distant chirps of crickets. Her makeshift bed was a pile of fallen leaves, providing a meagre barrier between her tired body and the unforgiving ground. As she sat there uncomfortably, she decided that her hunting expedition would begin after sunrise.

She wasn't quite sure where she would go after that; maybe a town, but then again, what if the people there proved to be just as hostile towards her? Albeit slowly, word of mouth travelled even over long distances, often passed on by wealthy travellers or merchants; it was likely that news about her would eventually reach other places. Evelyn could only hope that her tendency to lower her head in public would prove advantageous.

Despite her concerns and the odds being stacked against her, she knew that she had to press on. Her parents had made the ultimate sacrifice so that she could be free. She owed it to them not to take that for granted.

Chapter Three

Evelyn held her hands out in front of the fire and glanced up at the moon. Many days and nights had passed since the mob had taken her parents and forced her to flee her hometown.

Beside her was the lifeless body of a vole. She had caught it in one of the traps she'd set. She carefully picked it up and silently thanked it before setting it above the fire on a sharpened stick. She was careful to ensure that the flames licked around the body just enough to cook the meat slowly and evenly. Although the morsel was relatively small, and would not be a substantial meal by itself, the aroma of the cooked flesh filled the air, tantalising Evelyn's senses.

She continued to roast the vole until the skin was crispy. As she removed the stick from the flames, in her focus to quell her hunger, she felt a brief sense of relief settle upon her. Still musing on what her next move should be, she ate her food at a slow pace, appreciating the tender and succulent texture.

Feeling better for having consumed some protein, Evelyn rose to her feet and surveyed her environment. With its unbroken expanse of motionless trees, the forest was peaceful. Twinkling stars adorned the night sky, some peering through the veil of clouds. The lingering aroma of cooked meat from her food mingled with the earthy scent of deer and herbs. The surrounding cacophony of insect chirps served as a reminder of the forest's vibrant potential.

Cautious about the possible dangers of her identity being disclosed to another town, Evelyn was unaware of any alternative location to settle. She gazed up at the sky as the billowing smoke from the fire bloomed, polluting it. The irony wasn't lost on her that although fire had caused her so much loss, she would need to rely on it not only for warmth, but also, hopefully, as a means of aiding her search for a nearby town in the distance.

As a witch, although Evelyn's wounds could heal slightly faster than any ordinary human's, she could still feel their sharp sting. They served as a frequent reminder of the horror she'd fled, reinforcing her resolve to continue her travels; becoming ensnared in her thoughts of sorrow and discomfort would be a futile endeavour.

And so, she put out the fire, vowing to move forward.

As she walked around, surveying the area with hopes of locating civilisation, she was unsettled by the question of whether she wanted to take revenge on those who had wronged her. She tapped her chin with a grimy fingernail before shaking her head in dismissal. Pursuing vengeance would serve no purpose. Though she would permit herself to grieve, she relegated any notion of returning to her old town for revenge to the darkest corners of her mind.

Travelling past countless trees, Evelyn wasn't sure if she was heading in the right direction. She could only hope that wherever she found herself, she would not be in danger. Guided by the brightest star, she urged herself forward with every stride, persevering even through the toughest stretches of terrain.

Having lost track of how long she had been walking, Evelyn finally succumbed to exhaustion. With no adequate shelter around, the plummeting temperature made the outdoors increasingly hostile. She worried that hunting would become more difficult as more animals went into hibernation for the winter. She could set an infinite number of traps, all whilst increasing numbers of creatures wouldn't even be around to come across them. She was well aware that hunting in the coldest months of the year was a difficult task, even for the most experienced hunters. With only herself and her skills, she surmised that the odds were not in her favour. In the long run, to forage for merely berries and mushrooms would not be enough.

Too exhausted to search for even a humble alcove, Evelyn settled unceremoniously in a pile of leaves beneath a tree's shadow. She was too tired to be fazed by the insects that scuttled around. Although she could sense their tiny legs crawling on her skin, leaving sporadic pricks to indicate that they were nibbling her, they were the least of her worries. Her only concern was making it through to the next day.

Although she was sleepy, Evelyn's racing thoughts coaxed her gaze to scan the landscape. Suddenly, a plume of smoke billowing in the distance immediately caught her attention. The sight jolted her back to being fully alert. It was exactly what she had been hoping for. The mere indication of civilisation nearby filled her with a bright spark of enthusiasm.

Maybe this is my opportunity...

Too weak to immediately investigate the source of the smoke, Evelyn decided that a good night's rest was required. She needed it to rejuvenate her; it would help her to think more clearly about her next move. She needed to come up with a story – one that would sound believable enough to conceal her identity.

Who could I be? A noblewoman fleeing corruption? A mistreated servant who has finally taken a stand?

Both of those tales had an element of truth to them, but Evelyn still had her doubts. Her extensive scarring was a giveaway that something out of the ordinary had happened to her, but passing herself off as a rebel of some kind would not be convincing either. She swallowed hard, hoping that her appearance alone wouldn't arouse any suspicion.

***

Evelyn woke with a start. She was certain that something was amiss, but couldn't quite put her finger on it until she registered the gradually intensifying noise – the barking of an approaching hound.

"No! No, no, no!" she yelled out frenziedly.

Rising abruptly, she tripped and fell, but quickly regained her footing on the second attempt. She charged deeper into the forest. She bulldozed her way through the thicket, bumping into some of the trees, her evident fragility causing her to falter and struggle.

She felt a wave of despair wash over her as the dog's barking drew nearer, unrelenting in its pursuit. She thought back to the maniacal mob, driven by madness and poised to tear her apart. She couldn't bear the thought of meeting her end this way.

With her body no longer able to aid her escape, Evelyn curled up on the ground, petrified and gasping for air as tears streamed down her cheeks. She could only hope the dog wouldn't catch up to her, but fate had a different plan.

Suddenly emerging from the bushes, a large Doberman appeared. Much to Evelyn's surprise, it didn't seem at all aggressive; her shrieks of terror caused it to jump back. Trying to reassure her, the dog then came closer and nudged its wet nose against her face, but upon sensing her fear, it quickly whimpered and lowered its head while tucking its long tail between its legs.

Still shielding her face with her hands and curled up in a defensive ball, Evelyn didn't notice when the dog disappeared into the forest.

Eventually, sensing that the dog may have been trying to lead someone to her, Evelyn decided she needed to run. She tried to get up, but was too weary to do so, collapsing back onto the ground with a defeated groan of exasperation.

Her distress deepened upon the realisation that the hound wasn't finished with her yet. Emerging from the shadows, it appeared again, this time with a pheasant between its jaws. It was clear that the bird had been fatally shot by a hunter's arrow, its tanned feathers tarred with blood.

The dog dropped the pheasant and came plodding towards Evelyn. When it planted a sloppy kiss on her cheek with its wet tongue, she shuddered in disgust. Despite her efforts to get away, the dog remained dedicated in its attempts to get close to her.

"Bosun!" a female voice exclaimed urgently. "Leave her alone!"

Fright gripped Evelyn as she choked back sobs. She hadn't encountered another person since being chased out of her hometown by the angry mob. She had no idea what to expect and she was too exhausted and traumatised to assess whether they had the makings of a friend or foe.

As the newcomer approached, the large dog whimpered and abandoned Evelyn to return to the pheasant, bouncing around it with excitement.

"Hi there," the woman said to Evelyn in a gentle tone. "Sorry about that. Bosun's just excited because he's been hunting. You seem hurt. Is there anything I can do to help?"

Evelyn peeked out from between her fingers and saw a woman with long brown hair standing over her. She was dressed in hunting attire, consisting of a blend of leather and cotton garments which seemed to have been crafted with impeccable attention to detail. A bow and quiver hung from her back, and she carried a hunting knife on her belt. The expression on her pretty features was laced with mercy and concern.

A moment of quiet passed before the woman spoke once more.

"Don't worry. I mean you no harm. It seems like something terrible must have happened to make you act like this."

Crouching down beside Evelyn, the woman rummaged through a burlap sack and soon produced an apple. Unable to look away, Evelyn's hunger pangs intensified as she stared at the fruit. The woman noticed this and smiled warmly.

"Take it," she said softly.

Evelyn couldn't resist, and with trembling hands, reached out to take the apple. With a hungry look in her eyes, she devoured it in several bites. The sweet taste was like ambrosia on her tongue. Her gaze then shifted back to the kind woman. When their eyes met, the woman tilted her head inquisitively.

"I'm Zoey," she said.

Chapter Four

Initially, Evelyn didn't say a word. She could only tremble in silence. Zoey convinced her to take a seat on a tree trunk so she could be examined more closely. It was only through muttered words of faint protest that she eventually gave in.

Zoey started to assess Evelyn's injuries. She trailed the wounds with her finger, making sure that no infection had taken root. It was clear to her that Evelyn had suffered greatly, but she decided not to ask questions.

"I'm not surprised that you're anxious of Bosun," she observed at last. "You look like you've had a run-in with a pack of dogs – at least!"

At the sound of his name, Bosun pricked up his ears and bounded over to Zoey. However, before he could get too close, she motioned for him to stay put, her face set in a stern expression. His tail still wagged furiously though, eagerly awaiting the next command. Shaking her head endearingly, Zoey instructed her loyal companion to remain calm before turning her attention back to Evelyn.

"You need some help," she said, her tone kind but stern. "I don't know what's happened to you, but you can't make it through this alone – not for even another few nights. You look as though you haven't eaten a good meal in quite some time."

Evelyn glanced at her tired body, unable to deny that her ribs were protruding beneath the worn fabric of her clothes. She sniffled as she decided to accept Zoey's kindness. With the two of them being fairly similar in height, Zoey draped Evelyn's arm over her shoulder. They then proceeded across a field towards a nearby town, which was evident from the wisps of smoke that curled up into the night sky.

Evelyn practically jumped when the town came into view. Noticing the reaction right away, Zoey spoke in a gentle voice.

"It's ok. It's obvious you've been through something terrible. I won't let anyone hurt you. Let's get you to my place and see to it that you're fed."

Bosun walked devotedly by Zoey's side as she mused on what sort of meal to make with their catch. The happy pooch trotted along with his nose quivering at the aromas of food being cooked in several parts of the seemingly prosperous town. His tongue stuck out of his mouth as he looked around with a wagging tail. A thin layer of dust from the dirt road clung to his fur. Upon noticing this, Zoey made a promise to him.

"Good boy. I'll run the brush through your fur when we get home."

Bosun's feet leapt off the ground as he pranced at Zoey's side, his claws clacking against the cobblestones. It was as though he had understood her every word. With his nose to the ground, he then detected a morsel of meat that had probably been dropped by a merchant nearby. As he quickly moved to gobble it up, Evelyn watched him nervously. She found the innocence of his mannerisms reassuring, but still didn't feel completely at ease to be around a canine of any kind.

As they walked, several houses embellished with white paint and wooden beams came into view. The rustic dwellings had small fences in front of them, presumably for chickens to roam around during the daylight hours. Overall, the town was quite serene, even by night.

When they came across a certain shop, Zoey stopped to gaze into the glass window. She grinned at the sight of all the sparkling pieces of jewellery on display. Gemstones of different shapes and colours embedded in different metals glimmered radiantly, their forms bathed in a celestial glow, courtesy of the stars in the night sky. Evelyn slowly started to relax, and, becoming more comfortable in her new environment, felt at ease to converse with Zoey.

"There are so many beautiful things in there," she said. "I wouldn't know what to choose."

"This is my jewellery shop," Zoey said, her

voice tinged with a hint of pride. "It has taken me over ten years to build up this business. It requires my constant attention, but it's worth it. Wealthier patrons often come into town from far away to buy pieces here. The more common types of gems, which are just as beautiful, are popular with people on a more humble budget."

Noticing that Zoey appeared to be in her late twenties or early thirties, Evelyn assumed that she must have devoted herself to her work from a young age.

Evelyn walked with Zoey until they arrived at a house that seemed more spacious than the others. Built on top of a hill, it was next to another building with a tall chimney, wooden benches, and an overhang filled with various tools and hammers. Picking up on Evelyn's interest in it, Zoey offered an explanation.

"That's where I work my magic. The men who used to look down on me for being a female forgemaster and jewellery maker suddenly changed their tune when they realised the quality of my craftsmanship. I learnt everything I know from my father, who had an unrivalled expertise in the industry."

Zoey stumbled over her words a little when she spoke of her father. Although Evelyn noticed it, she decided not to pry.

"Anyway," said Zoey. "We're here now. Please, make yourself at home."

As soon as they entered Zoey's home, she closed the door behind them, shutting out the crisp chill of the air outside. Inside, the atmosphere was pleasant. Zoey gestured to a cosy chair. Evelyn gratefully embraced its comfort, which was wonderfully superior to the mere ground she had been sleeping on. The reassuring environment soon caused her to let her guard down; though she wasn't that well acquainted with Zoey, she knew it would be foolish to reject the help of someone who seemed so honest and welcoming.

Zoey worked to prepare the pheasant, plucking its feathers and getting a fire going. Evelyn almost drifted off to sleep, but forced herself to stay awake. Instead, she watched Zoey move around, admiring how her muscles seemed to ripple as she worked.

Instinctively aware of the tension that radiated from her, Bosun avoided getting too close to Evelyn. He shot her an occasional defeated glance before settling down into a pile of animal furs. He cradled a femur bone that had been stripped of its meat. Later, Zoey brought him a bowl of pheasant stew and offered one to Evelyn as well, handing it to her tenderly.

"Here you go," she said as she gave Evelyn a spoon. "This is full of protein. I hope it will help you, if only a bit."

With the bowl of stew cradled in her hands, Evelyn inhaled deeply, savouring the rich aroma that wafted up from the heat-laden concoction. The tantalising scent filled her senses, a stark contrast to the meagre provisions of the forest. As she brought the spoon to her lips, the first taste sent a wave of satisfaction through her. The flavours, a symphony of herbs and spices, unfolded on her palate, each new spoonful a revelation. The tender chunks of meat and hearty vegetables were a feast of sheer pleasure, a welcome departure from the survival rations of the wilderness.

Evelyn gazed up at Zoey. She couldn't find the words to express her gratitude, especially as thoughts of the nights she'd spent out in the elements flashed through her mind.

"Once you've finished your stew, I could run you a bath if you like."

"Evelyn."

"Huh?"

"I didn't tell you my name. It's Evelyn."

"It's a pleasure to meet you," said Zoey, her face lighting up with a smile. "Let's take care of your wounds. I have a herbal mixture that can help to keep them from getting infected. Even though some of your cuts have already closed up, it's still a good idea to take preventative measures."

Evelyn expressed her approval with a nod of her head.

"I couldn't see any signs of infection at first glance," Zoey added. "But I'd like to double-check, just to be sure."

Zoey prepared the bath by starting a fire in the pit underneath. The wood crackled and spat in the vibrant embers, slowly giving the water a desirable warmth. As steam began to rise, she gave a satisfied nod, certain that everything would soon be ready.

After adding some salts and calming lavender and camomile, she directed her attention back to Evelyn, who had now finished eating. She helped her undress and examined her wounds again. After everything she'd been through, Evelyn felt at ease with Zoey's touch.

"My expertise doesn't extend to wounds," Zoey said. "If I come across something serious, we might have to see a medic. Hopefully though, everything should be fine if you continue to heal properly."

As soon as Zoey had helped her into the bath, Evelyn carefully lowered herself into the water. Every muscle in her body relaxed for the first time since the frenzied mob had come running. She could smell the soothing aromas as she closed her eyes and felt a cloth being hung on her arm. As she ran it over her body, she had no need to feel shy; Zoey had already moved away to wash-up their empty bowls.

Submerged in the soothing heat, as Evelyn relaxed, the water around her began to take on a reddish hue, tainted by the remnants of her wounds. The once-clear bathwater now mirrored the struggles she had faced. The blood and mud mingling in the water served as a stark reminder.

Once Evelyn had finished bathing, Zoey stood tactfully with a thick blanket outstretched for her to step into. With a nod and a smile, Evelyn appreciatively accepted it, wrapping it around her tired body.

"I don't have a spare bed," said Zoey. "Let me know if you need extra blankets or pillows for the furniture though."

"The furniture is comfortable," Evelyn replied. "You've been so good to me. I can't thank you enough."

"You're welcome. Everyone needs a friend and it's clear that you were struggling out there on your own. Oh, and by the way, I'm sorry if Bosun scared you. He can be very excitable, but he means well."

Although Zoey's expression was serene and

reassuring, Evelyn drew in a deep breath, distracted by the lingering discomfort from the bite on her arm. She managed to smile, though she knew she would need to recover physically just as much as mentally. Her gaze rested on Bosun, who lay still with his bone between his paws, breathing in and out peacefully. He looked so innocent, vulnerable, and certainly not menacing at all.

"He's a good boy," Evelyn said. "I need to remember that not all dogs are a threat."

As the first glimmers of morning light began to filter in through the windows, Evelyn yawned.

"Let's get some sleep," said Zoey. "It's been a long night for both of us."

Evelyn drifted in and out of a fitful sleep, the terror of her nightmares refusing to let her rest. She tossed and turned in her comfortable makeshift bed, crying out from time to time as the visions of her ordeal filled her mind. Whenever she woke from the most upsetting dreams, there was Zoey, holding her hand with a gentle expression and soothing voice. Her presence was a reminder that someone still cared, that someone good was there for her.

"I can feel the turmoil in your soul, Evelyn. Do you want me to stay with you for a bit? Maybe it will help. It's no trouble for me to sit here and read a book. You're safe with me. We hardly know each other, but I'm determined to get you well again."

Evelyn nodded in humble acceptance of Zoey's considerate offer. It calmed her enough to numb the impact of her bad dreams, helping her to get through a day's sleep. Although she had gone through so much, Zoey's kindness inspired her to believe that maybe there was hope after all, and that perhaps she could make it from the darkness into the light.

Would Zoey still be kind to me if she knew about me being a witch? I don't want to lie to her, but now doesn't feel like the right time to mention it.

Chapter Five

Evelyn stumbled through the smoke, desperately seeking an escape. She had no idea which way to go, and her eyes stung so much that she could barely make out shapes. All around her, the world was being consumed by flames. Her throat burned and her body felt heavy, making each step slower and more laboured.

The heat and smoke was overwhelming. Evelyn felt her lungs begin to close. Tears spilled down her face as she coughed and struggled for breath. Through the cracking embers, she could hear her mother's panicked screams. Each breath felt like a battle, and she fought desperately to stay conscious.

The smell of burning flesh was everywhere. Evelyn's mind kept returning to her father's death. She could see it playing out, again and again.

She felt someone shaking her shoulders, and she tried to fight them off. But the person persisted. When she opened her eyes, she could see Zoey staring back at her, speaking in a soft voice as though trying to soothe an injured animal.

"It's ok, Evelyn. You're safe. Nobody can hurt you here. Take some deep breaths."

Evelyn took Zoey's advice and was soon able to relax, much to Zoey's relief.

"You were having another nightmare," Zoey explained. "I had to take immediate action to stop you from sinking further into despair. You were so consumed by it."

"Oh?" Evelyn mused in shock and disbelief, disappointed that the nightmares had won once again.

She sat up and slumped forward in defeat. The moonlight coming in from outside revealed that it was now nighttime. Zoey had been taking care of her for three days, constantly bringing her food in the hope of aiding her recovery. During this time, the nightmares had been frequent.

Zoey, seeming to sense Evelyn's frustration, stepped forward and gently placed a bowl of soup on the table next to her. Evelyn groaned and rubbed her forehead, her eyes half-closed in exhaustion. Zoey stayed quiet, gesturing for her to eat. Evelyn hesitantly picked up the spoon and began to scoop some of the hot, soothing broth into her mouth.

The soup was surprisingly comforting. Evelyn could feel the heat radiating through her body as it filled her empty stomach. She savoured the taste, letting the warmth and peace of the moment sink in. She looked up to see Zoey smiling kindly.

"Good," Zoey said. "You need the nutrition for your mind as well as for your body."

Zoey settled gracefully into the chair beside Evelyn, her movements deliberate, yet graceful. Seizing an opportunity to offer comfort, she reached for a hairbrush from the nearby table. She then ran the soft bristles through Evelyn's hair with a rhythmic, soothing motion. Evelyn appreciatively surrendered to the gentle strokes.

"I'm sure I can untangle the worst of the knots," Zoey said. "I bet your hair normally looks lovely."

Despite enjoying the sensations of having her hair brushed, Evelyn almost choked on her soup when Bosun slowly came over. He sadly looked up at her, sensing her unease. She peered at him cautiously while rubbing her arm and leaning back and away from him. Zoey cleared her throat, prompting the dog to obey her hand signal to stay back.

"Good boy," she said gently.

"It's ok," said Evelyn. "I know he means well. I must learn to trust him."

She glanced down at the teeth marks on her arm, and Bosun whined softly as if sensing her distress. Tentatively, she extended her hand towards him, and he perked up his ears and tilted his head in interest. His tail began to thump slowly against the floor as he crept closer, sniffing at her fingers before nuzzling into her palm. Evelyn held her breath as she cautiously stroked his fur, feeling a sense of comfort from the hound's warmth and affection. After a few moments, she withdrew her hand, but not before giving him one final pet on the head.

Bosun barked joyfully and pounced onto his bed of neatly-arranged furs. Evelyn grinned sheepishly, glancing at Zoey, who had finished brushing her hair and was now leaning against the far wall, observing the scene before her.

"From the marks on your arm, you've got every right to be scared of dogs," she said. "Even though you don't have to, I'm proud of you for giving Bosun a chance."

Evelyn nodded and smiled. As she gazed around the room, she noticed that the walls of the house were a deep chestnut hue, glowing in the light from the open fire as smoke slowly drifted out of the chimney. Her eyes lit up at the sight of jewels glistening on a shelf near the flames. Zoey noticed her gaze and let out an amused chuckle.

"Once you're up to it, I can show you the

forge," she said proudly. "There's no rush though. I can't pretend that I'm not tempted to involve you in my work – only if you'd want that, of course."

Throughout the remainder of the night, the two of them talked more. Evelyn made a conscious decision to steer clear of discussing her parents, and instead directed the conversation towards more positive experiences, such as reminiscing about her excursions into the forest and learning how to hunt.

"That's how I managed to survive in the wilderness before you found me," Evelyn finished, her tone carrying a note of assurance.

"That's amazing!" Zoey said gleefully as she clapped her hands together. "I always knew you were a woman of great strength, Evelyn. Being self-sufficient is such a valuable skill."

With a shy grin, Evelyn rubbed her cheek and slowly rose to her feet, prompting a sharp glance from Zoey.

"I need to build up my strength," Evelyn said.

"Simply sitting around won't help me in that. Besides, I'd like to repay your kindness by helping you out around here."

"Ok," said Zoey. "You have to promise me that you won't push yourself too hard though. If there's something that feels like it's too much, you must ask me to do it. I insist."

***

After a few days, as she began to regain some strength, Evelyn opened up to Zoey a bit more. Zoey was only aware of bits and pieces from Evelyn's past, but she refrained from prying and trusted that Evelyn would divulge the full story at her own pace. Zoey was content that Evelyn didn't owe her an explanation and was a good person.

Evelyn followed Zoey eagerly, a few paces behind as they headed into the forge. There were tools and materials everywhere – some of them familiar, some of them mysterious, but all of them reflecting Zoey's passion and creativity. Evelyn watched patiently as Zoey stoked the fire until it roared to life, the heat filling the room.

As she approached the workbench, Zoey glanced back over her shoulder at Evelyn, her expression bright with anticipation as she reached for her apron and began to line up her tools in an order that made sense only to her.

"I'll talk you through what I'm doing as I work," Zoey explained.

Zoey's face was a mask of concentration as she moved from task to task, her movements fluid and swift. The process lasted for several hours as she toiled away. Covered in sweat and grime, her hard work paid off. She managed to craft a beautiful, simple silver band with an emerald at the centre. Evelyn observed intently the entire time, and upon seeing the finished product, examined it with keen interest.

Astounded by Zoey's expertise, Evelyn felt a pang of regret that she hadn't spent more time honing her own skills over the years.

"You're a hard worker," she murmured.

Zoey smiled and shrugged humbly.

"I have to be," she said. "Times can be tough. My father taught me to never crumble under pressure. Instead, I learnt to rise to the challenge and be self-reliant. In a world where individuals like myself can be viewed as inferior, I chose to take control of my life and lead it independently."

"You're empowered," Evelyn said, unable to stifle her admiration. "I regret not having strived for something similar when I had the opportunity."

"Maybe you could be my apprentice," Zoey suggested.

Evelyn looked at her intently, searching for any indication of sarcasm. Not finding any, she tilted her head slightly.

"Really? Are you sure?"

"Absolutely!" Zoey answered enthusiastically. "I can recognise a strong spirit when I see one; it would be great to have you working with me."

Evelyn felt honoured. She promised herself that she would share her past and secret with

Zoey in due time. She wasn't sure when that would be though. To reveal her identity as a witch wasn't the sort of thing that could be taken back if it didn't go well. Her stomach tightened at the thought. Would Zoey hate her if she knew the truth? The more she considered it, the more it dawned on her that she was becoming attached to Zoey. It made her all the more anxious about the possibility of rejection.

Chapter Six

A week later, as Evelyn sat calmly on a hill overlooking Zoey's town, she was appreciative of how much stronger she was feeling. Zoey had been feeding her well with the most nutritious of meals.

She still hadn't found the strength to tell Zoey the truth about her identity. She remained torn between the desire to be honest, and the fear of rejection. She knew she couldn't keep the truth hidden forever, but all the same, she hadn't found the right moment in which to speak. Even the thought of the conversation was enough to make her heart race.

Gazing up at the stars, Evelyn lifted her index finger and traced some of the constellations overhead. The sky was so clear compared to the starless midnight she had endured when smoke from the mob's torches had billowed into the sky, blackening the night.

Upon hearing the rustling of leaves from behind, she tensed, her body becoming rigid. Suddenly, a hound emerged, causing her to let out a gasp. However, as soon as she recognised Bosun, a wave of relief washed over her. She was working on becoming more at ease with him, but was still prone to moments where her anxiety consumed her.

Sensing that he must have unsettled Evelyn, Bosun backed away. Despite his wariness, his tail continued to wag. He placidly sat down, sniffing the air incessantly.

With Bosun around, Evelyn suspected that Zoey would be nearby. Surely enough, her smile broadened as she heard footsteps and saw Zoey emerging from the darkness. Bosun rushed over to rest his head on Zoey as she sat down next to Evelyn. Zoey stroked his head tenderly, taking a moment to appreciate the peacefulness of the evening. Inhaling deeply, she savoured the crispness of the air against the tranquillity of the landscape.

"I want to sit with you and stargaze," Zoey

said. "Sometimes you seem rather quiet, and I want to make sure you're doing alright. We haven't got long before it gets too cold, so once we're back in the house, I'll start a fire and prepare a nice hot meal."

Reassured by Zoey's words, Evelyn nodded in agreement. They watched the sky contentedly as a few clouds drifted across the stars.

"It feels as though it will snow soon," said Evelyn, not wishing to talk about herself.

"Indeed," said Zoey. "I'm not too worried. We'll be fine. I've got plenty of salted meat in the cellar. Besides, the winter can be harsh, but it doesn't have to be lonely. You can stay here with me for as long as you need – if you'd like to, of course."

A pang of guilt churned in Evelyn's stomach as she realised she hadn't done much to lend a hand. With a quizzical expression, she glanced at Zoey.

"That's such a kind offer. Are you sure? I haven't really done anything to earn my keep."

"It's ok," Zoey said gently. "You don't owe me anything. If you need to head off and be somewhere else, you have my full understanding and support. That said, even with Bosun here, it can get rather lonely without another human in the house. I enjoy your company and it would be a pleasure to share my resources with you over the winter. You're welcome to stay for as long as you like."

Having heard the mention of his name, Bosun became alert, his tongue hanging out of his mouth as he playfully tilted his head. Even though he didn't understand what was being said, he was pleased to be acknowledged. He wagged his tail as Zoey continued to stroke his head, causing some strands of fur to be blown away in the wind.

As she observed the heartwarming exchange between Zoey and Bosun, Evelyn made a firm decision to put more effort into overcoming her fear of the dog. It was evident that the two were close companions and that Bosun was far from being an aggressive creature. Evelyn was confident that with time, she would be able to conquer her apprehension. She turned to Zoey with a smile, feeling grateful for her kindness and understanding.

"I would love to stay with you and Bosun," she said. "I have to be honest though; I'm not quite ready to venture out into the town just yet. It's going to take some time for me to feel safe going out again."

Zoey had no desire to pry, and so, the two women continued to converse for a little while longer, sharing stories with one another. As usual, Zoey took the lead in the conversation, but it was something that Evelyn welcomed.

As the temperature dropped, they rose to their feet and started to walk, with Bosun following alongside. Evelyn felt a shiver run through her body, not from the chill in the air, but due to her thoughts drifting back to the hidden parts of herself that she hadn't revealed to Zoey.

"Do you ever wonder about the supernatural?" she asked, breaking the moment's silence.

Zoey pondered the question for a while before answering.

"I think stuff like that probably does exist,"

she said. "I don't fear it though. I think if there was something that I needed to be wary of, Bosun would let me know. He's a great judge of character. I'm more scared of people than whatever else might be out there, Evelyn. I think they're probably the real threat."

Pleasantly surprised by Zoey's perspective, and a little taken aback, Evelyn was quiet as they walked back home. As soon as they got inside, she set about tidying up whilst Zoey gave Bosun a marrowbone. Soon after, Zoey began preparing dinner by skinning a pigeon and adding root vegetables to the pot. The meal would serve as a necessary staple for the cold night. Watching Zoey cook reminded Evelyn of the winters she'd spent with her parents before they were taken from her.

After dinner, everyone said goodnight and got settled in their respective sleeping spots. Evelyn's mind remained busy though. She found herself grappling with the unexpected revelation Zoey had shared. It was a touch reassuring that someone as wise as Zoey could view the supernatural with something other than fear and hatred. However, whilst Evelyn appreciated Zoey's open-mindedness, she knew she couldn't take it for granted that everything would be fine upon her revealing her identity as a witch.

Left with more questions than answers, Evelyn succumbed to an exhausted yawn as her body prepared itself for sleep.

80

Chapter Seven

In the weeks that passed, Evelyn and Zoey grew closer. Evelyn had become more comfortable in talking about her family; the stories she shared had more details than before. Her sadness that her parents were no longer alive was evident, but Zoey didn't press further on the matter.

Zoey walked up to Bosun and softly stroked his head.

"Good boy," she said.

Seated across from Bosun, Evelyn observed him from a cautious distance. The mere presence of the dog triggered a wave of apprehension in her, but she was determined to overcome her fear. With a deliberate gentleness, she extended her hand towards Bosun, her movements slow, yet certain. The dog, sensing her nervous energy, regarded her with an expression that was both curious and cautious. Evelyn's heart raced, but she maintained a reassuring smile.

"Hey, Bosun," she whispered, her voice carrying a mixture of trepidation and kindness. "It's ok, buddy. We're friends, right?"

Bosun, ever perceptive, seemed to sense the sincerity in Evelyn's gesture. His tail, initially poised in watchfulness, began to wag. He then came and stood next to her, calmly letting her brush her fingers against the soft fur on his back. The initial tension began to dissolve, to be replaced by a shared understanding.

Zoey leapt up joyously, clapping her hands in celebration.

"Well done, Evelyn," she said. "I know it's taken a lot to get past your fear. It means the world to me that you're doing your utmost to welcome Bosun with open arms."

Evelyn rose from her seat and watched as the hound went back to his bed to chew on a bone. She put her hand on Zoey's shoulder before speaking.

"I couldn't have done that without you."

"May I give you a hug?" Zoey asked.

Evelyn gave a resolute nod, prompting Zoey to throw her arms wide, almost as if she was about to take flight. The two women then held each other in a fervent embrace, clinging to one another in appreciation of their close bond.

They gave each other a final friendly squeeze before Evelyn stepped back.

"Now that I'm getting over more of my fears, I'd quite like to go out more," she said. "Maybe not into the town straight away, but perhaps we could go to the forest – just for a final hunt before the season's weather takes a turn for the worst."

"That's a wonderful idea," Zoey replied with enthusiasm. "We're not short on supplies, but I wouldn't say no to the fresh air, especially if it means helping you overcome your fears. Now that you're more comfortable with Bosun, I'm sure we'll make an amazing team."

***

Evelyn followed Zoey through the dense forest. The trees towered above them, casting long shadows over the ground. The sound of birds chirping and leaves rustling filled her ears, and the fresh smell of pine filled her nose. It had been too long since she'd been outside like this.

Bosun bounded happily ahead of them, his nose to the ground as he sniffed for any signs of prey.

Zoey turned around to check that Evelyn was doing ok.

"Don't worry," she said, her voice soft and soothing. "You're safe with me."

Evelyn smiled humbly. Although she was a confident hunter herself and had enjoyed walks alone in the forest back home, her confidence had taken a knock after everything that had happened that terrible night. There was something about being with

Zoey that she had come to rely upon. There was something about Zoey that made her feel at ease. Maybe it was the way she always seemed to know what to do in any situation, or maybe it was just her assured and friendly demeanour that made Evelyn feel like everything was going to be ok.

All the same, as they walked deeper into the forest, Evelyn couldn't help but feel a sense of unease. It seemed to be getting darker and quieter – the only sound was the crunching of leaves beneath their feet. Certain that she was being paranoid, she tried to push the feeling aside and focus on enjoying the fresh air.

Suddenly, Bosun's ears perked up as he let out a low growl. In response, Zoey crept forward, her bow at the ready, signalling for Evelyn to stay back. Evelyn held her breath, watching as Zoey followed Bosun into the bushes, the pair of them disappearing out of her sight.

As she stood by the edge of the clearing on her own, Evelyn folded her arms across her chest. She shifted her weight from one foot to the other. She kept telling herself that she needed to keep still, but impatience was getting the better of her. Time seemed to stretch on like an infinite thread, weaving through the moments with an almost deliberate languor.

Where are they? It shouldn't be taking them this long.

As a hunter herself, Evelyn knew there was something wrong. It was in her gut; a feeling of unease that wouldn't go away.

Every moment that passed only served to heighten her anxiety. Despite her efforts to stay calm, her mind conjured up all sorts of scenarios. What if Zoey and Bosun had been ambushed by a pack of wolves? What if they were injured and unable to move? The longer they were gone, the more Evelyn's imagination ran wild.

Her heart raced as she considered going after her friends. But she knew better than to rush blindly into danger. She needed to stay put and wait for them to return.

All of a sudden, Zoey burst out from the bushes. She didn't have Bosun with her, and her face was streaked with tears.

"Zoey, what's wrong?" Evelyn asked, her voice shaking.

Zoey gasped for breath, trying to compose herself.

"Bosun... something terrible has happened to Bosun," she finally managed to say between sobs.

Chapter Eight

"Where is he?" Evelyn asked, her voice rising in panic. "What's happened?"

"I don't know," Zoey answered, her voice thick with distress. "Bosun was behind me and then I sensed that he'd stopped walking. I turned around to see him on his side on the ground. As far as I know, he's still there. I tried to get him to move, but he seems too weak to get up. I even tried to lift him, but he was too heavy."

Zoey motioned for Evelyn to follow her. They began making their way through the bushes to find Bosun. It was dense with ferns and brambles that snagged at their clothes and scratched their skin. Not only did the abundance of overgrowth make the short journey difficult – it made it harder for the two women to see far ahead. They had to push aside branches and leaves just to make their way through.

As soon as Evelyn spotted Bosun, she could sense that he wasn't well. He was panting abnormally fast, and his tongue was hanging out of his mouth, which looked exceptionally dry. Her heart sank as she saw him struggling to catch his breath.

Zoey ran up to Bosun and put her hand on his side.

"Come on, boy. I don't know what's wrong, but please, *please* be ok."

Too weak to even lift his head, the poor soul whined in response.

Evelyn knelt down next to Zoey. The situation was too urgent for her to feel any fear towards the dog. Instead, she examined him carefully, running a cautious hand over his body. When she got to his front paws, she paused, observing thoughtfully.

"I think he's been bitten by a snake," she said, pointing to a small puncture wound on Bosun's paw.

"We need to get him some help," Zoey exclaimed, her eyes widening. "But what can we do? We're in the middle of nowhere."

The irony of the situation wasn't lost on Evelyn. Once again she was faced with the same dilemma that had seemingly cost her so dearly back home.

If I don't help Bosun, he will die. The poison from the snake is quickly taking over his body. I don't even have time to think about this.

Evelyn knew that in choosing to heal Bosun, her identity as a witch would be immediately revealed to Zoey. Equally though, there was no way that she was willing to let Zoey lose her beloved pet.

Accepting that her own fate was out of her hands, Evelyn took a deep breath and decided to take charge.

"I'm going to help him," she told Zoey. "Stand back and let me work."

"How are you going to..."

"Trust me," Evelyn said with confidence.

Confused, but willing to put her faith in her friend, Zoey stood back. Terrified of losing Bosun, all she could do was watch and hope, her face contorted with worry.

As Evelyn bent forward to take a closer look at Bosun's paw, she could see that it was becoming increasingly swollen and discoloured. The poison was already coursing through his veins, and time was running out.

Focusing her energy, Evelyn began to tune into her powers. She placed her hand on Bosun's paw and whispered an incantation under her breath, calling upon the magic that had been passed down through her family for generations.

A soft, warm glow began to emanate from her palm, growing brighter and brighter until it enveloped the entire area around Bosun's paw. The light then expanded around Bosun's whole body, its glow illuminating the forest as it shimmered.

The magic flowing from Evelyn into Bosun seemed to pulse and throb with a life of its own; the very essence of her being flowed from her fingertips, radiating its way into

Bosun's body like a soothing balm. The air around them crackled with energy, as if they were at the centre of a powerful storm.

As the light intensified, Bosun's breathing began to steady. His body relaxed, as if he had fallen into a deep, comforting sleep. Evelyn could sense the poison being neutralised, and knew that her magic was working to heal his paw and restore him to health.

Watching from the sidelines, Zoey's face was a picture of shock and fascination. She couldn't take her eyes off the mesmerising display. Although she didn't understand the full extent of what was happening, she was in awe of it.

And then, just as suddenly as it had appeared, the light surrounding Bosun withdrew itself from him and moved back to Evelyn, who looked serene and in control. As the light all around her began to fade and resume its location in just the palm of her hand, she withdrew her touch from Bosun. With her hand extended in front of her, the final ball of light disappeared with a faint pop, leaving behind a peaceful silence, broken only by the sound of Bosun's soft breathing. Although still weak, he managed to look up at her in acknowledgment, indicating an improvement in his condition.

Evelyn turned around to look at Zoey, who was still staring in disbelief with a mixture of amazement and wonder.

"That was incredible," Zoey exclaimed. "You've saved him."

With his breathing back to normal, and with his paw having returned to its regular size and colour, Zoey rushed over to Bosun and scooped his head up in her arms. Overwhelmed with relief and love for him, she planted several kisses on the softest part of his cheek.

"What... What just happened?" she stammered, still struggling to process what she had just seen.

"I promise I was going to tell you," Evelyn said, still afraid of upsetting her friend. "It's just that I haven't been able to find the right moment to tell you and..."

"You're a witch?" Zoey interjected, cautiously, but keen for an answer.

"Yes," Evelyn said. "I'm so sorry."

"We'll talk later," said Zoey. "Let's get Bosun home."

Chapter Nine

Evelyn and Zoey made their way back through the town, with Bosun happily trotting along beside them. The windows of the thatched-roofed homes glowed with the warm light of candles and fires within.

Zoey was practically bouncing with joy, her heart light with relief that Bosun was going to be alright. She couldn't stop petting him at every possible interval, her fingers running through his soft fur as she paused to whisper words of affection into his ear.

Meanwhile, Evelyn was lost in thought. Although she was happy that Bosun was ok, she couldn't shake the unease about the looming conversation. She had known for a while that it couldn't be avoided, but it didn't make the thought of it any easier.

As they walked, Evelyn couldn't help but glance over at Zoey every so often, wondering how she was going to explain everything to her, and what the consequences might be.

Apart from the echo of their footsteps on the cobblestones, the town was quiet. The night sky was clear and starry, the air crisp and cool. In the distance, a shimmering crescent moon glowed like a beacon, but still Evelyn's mind raced with thoughts of how to find the words to explain herself without scaring or upsetting Zoey.

When they reached the house, Zoey turned to Evelyn, her eyes bright with gratitude.

"Thank you, Evelyn. I don't know what I would have done without you."

Evelyn smiled, trying to push aside her worries for the moment.

"You're welcome," she said. "I'm just glad I could help."

As they stepped inside the cosy home, Bosun bounding ahead of them, Evelyn couldn't shake her lingering feeling of dread.

"Let's get settled in first," Zoey said.

There was no malice or coldness in her tone. It was clear to Evelyn that Zoey simply wanted to get comfortable for the night after the long day they'd had.

Zoey busied herself in the kitchen, the savoury aroma from the pot of stew wafting through the air as she buttered some fresh bread.

Meanwhile, Bosun had settled into his bed, his tail thumping contentedly against the floor. Zoey walked over to him and gave him a tender pat on the head before placing a plate of meat in front of him; she wanted him to have the extra nourishment after his ordeal in the forest.

Sitting at the small kitchen table, Evelyn watched as Zoey went back to the stove. She admired her friend's ability to find comfort in simple things, even in the face of difficult circumstances.

With no job to do, and amidst the silence, Evelyn fidgeted with her hands, her mind racing with worry about the conversation she knew they needed to have. She had been putting it off for too long, and now that Zoey knew she was a witch, she knew it was time to explain to her the reasons why she had kept it hidden for so long.

"It's not much, but it'll warm us up," Zoey said happily of the meal she was making.

Evelyn nodded, grateful for the distraction.

"That sounds wonderful. Thank you."

Zoey bustled about the kitchen, humming a tune under her breath as she stirred the pot. The sound filled the air, along with the soft crackle of the fire in the hearth.

As they ate their dinner, the warmth of the stew spreading through their bodies, Zoey spoke about her love for the town, mentioning some of the quirks of the quaint landmarks they had passed on their way home from the forest.

Evelyn listened with interest, admiring Zoey's gentle nature and the fact that she seemed so at ease in the circumstances. It didn't seem as though Zoey was trying to gloss over something important with dismissive small talk. Instead, it struck Evelyn that she simply still felt comfortable around her.

Once they'd finished their meal, Zoey cleared the table and then returned, facing Evelyn and ready to talk.

"Ok," she said. "Tell me as much or as little as you're comfortable with. I promised myself that I wouldn't pry or put you on the spot, and I stand by that. It's just that now I know you're a witch, I want you to know that I accept you as you are, and if there's anything else you ever want to talk about, I'm on your side. It takes a lot to shock or offend me, and as I mentioned before, the real worry in this world is not often from a source of the supernatural. Oh... by the way, are you ok with that word, 'supernatural'?"

"You're being so sweet about this," Evelyn answered, pleasantly surprised.

She sensed that Zoey had been rambling through fear of upsetting her, or perhaps through a lack of experience with witches. It was, after all, uncommon for normals to be familiar with witches due to their need to keep a low profile.

"I've always been afraid to tell you I'm a witch," Evelyn explained. "I didn't want you to reject me for it."

"I could never reject you," Zoey insisted, her expression firm. "You're my friend, and I care about you no matter what. Why were you so scared to tell me?"

"I come from a town where witches are hunted and killed," Evelyn said, her voice low and laced with sadness. "I've seen some terrible things. All my life, I've had to keep my identity a secret. The day I failed to do so back home, was the day that I sealed mine and my parents' fate."

"Your parents?"

Evelyn took a deep breath before continuing.

"When the townspeople found out about my parents and I being witches, they accused us of all sorts of terrible things," she said. "They called us evil, and assumed we worshiped the devil."

Zoey's expression turned to one of shock and horror.

"That's terrible," she said, placing a hand on Evelyn's shoulder in comfort.

"It was," Evelyn agreed. "One night, they came to our home with torches and pitchforks, screaming for us to come out. They accused us of using our magic to harm their crops and their livestock, which was completely untrue."

"What happened next?" Zoey asked, her features widening with worry.

Evelyn swallowed hard as she tried to choke back her tears.

"They killed my parents right in front of me," she said with a lump in her throat as she stifled back a sob. "And then they turned on me. I had no choice but to run for my life."

Zoey was silent for a moment as she endeavoured to process everything that Evelyn had just told her.

"It's dreadful that anyone could be so cruel,"

she finally said. "I'm so sorry, Evelyn. You've been through so much."

"So now you know the truth about me," Evelyn said, tears streaming down her face. "I wasn't planning to keep it from you forever; I've just been so scared to tell you."

"Thank you for trusting me enough to tell me," Zoey answered, her voice filled with emotion. "I'm here for you, no matter what. We'll get through this together."

"I've always been so afraid that people would judge me and reject me because of who I am," Evelyn continued. "You've been so nice to me and I couldn't bear the thought of you hating me too."

"I could never hate you. You're safe here with me. You don't have to hide who you are anymore. Besides, I can't thank you enough for saving Bosun. You healed him with your magic. I've always had a strong feeling that you are a kind soul, and what you did for Bosun and I today has proved my instincts right."

Grateful for Zoey's acceptance and

understanding, Evelyn felt a weight lift off her shoulders. For the first time in a long time, she felt like she truly belonged somewhere.

"You know that night I found you all alone in the forest," said Zoey. "Was that after the mob had chased you from your hometown?"

"Yes," Evelyn replied, a hint of shame in her tone. "I'd spent several nights outdoors by then."

"No wonder you were so exhausted," Zoey reasoned. "I'm glad I found you when I did."

"I was in such a bad way," Evelyn admitted. "You saved me. Witches can't self-heal."

"I'm just happy to have helped," said Zoey.

"Thank you," said Evelyn, touched by Zoey's kindness.

"And don't feel bad that it took you so long to tell me the truth," Zoey added. "I appreciate that it must have been hard for you after everything you've been through."

The two women sat quietly for a while. The silence was comfortable, reflective of a shared empathy. As though sensing that he was needed in that moment, Bosun padded over to the table, his tail wagging happily. Playfully nuzzling his head against Evelyn's leg, he looked up at her with big puppy-dog eyes.

Evelyn smiled down at him and ran her hand over his soft fur.

"Hey there, Bosun," she said affectionately. "I'm glad you're feeling better."

Bosun responded with an excited bark, his tail wagging even harder. He then put his chin on Evelyn's lap and breathed out a slow, contented sigh.

"I think he's trying to say thank you," Zoey said proudly. "He must know that it was you who saved him."

"I'm honoured," said Evelyn. "He's a lovely boy."

"I'm glad you're not scared of him anymore."

"The mob chased me with hounds," Evelyn explained. "Bosun is nothing like any of them. I see that now. I wonder though, has he known all along that I'm a witch?"

"That's an interesting question," said Zoey. "I guess we'll never know. That said, I'm convinced Bosun can sense if someone has a good soul. I believe that very deeply. He once chased a man out of the shop. It turned out later that he'd pocketed a few chains – nothing too expensive, mind, but a theft all the same. Bosun must have known he was up to no good. His hackles were practically up the second the robber entered the shop."

"That's amazing," said Evelyn.

"And anyway," said Zoey, "what makes you think that being a witch makes you a bad person?"

Evelyn had to think long and hard about Zoey's question. She had never thought about it before. It took her a while to come up with an answer.

"I'm not sure," she said. "I suppose having grown up in a town where my family and I knew of other witches being hunted and killed, we just took it for granted that to be a witch is to be lesser in some way: less worthy, less deserving – a problem and a blight on the community."

"And yet the people who made you feel that way were the real monsters," Zoey said, frowning and deep in thought.

"I'd never thought of it like that, but perhaps you're right," said Evelyn. "I've never used my magic to hurt anyone, and yet normals on a witch hunt are some of the most violent types I've ever seen."

"Exactly," said Zoey, pleased that Evelyn was beginning to question the mentality that had worked so sorely against her. "You're a kind, thoughtful person, Evelyn – and one that just happens to be a witch as well. I hope that maybe one day, you can find the peace and self-acceptance you deserve."

The two women looked contentedly down at Bosun, who was now lying comfortably at their feet. His body moved with the steady, soothing rhythm of his breathing.

Zoey let out a yawn and stretched her arms above her head.

"Let's get some sleep," she said. "It's been a long day, and we both need our rest."

After Zoey had gone up to bed, Evelyn got settled amongst the pillows and furs on the furniture, appreciating the warmth and comfort of everything surrounding her. As exhaustion started to take over her body and mind, she entered one of the most restful slumbers that she'd had in a long time.

Chapter Ten

Several months had passed. Summertime was approaching and would soon bring an abundance of plentiful supplies. Having embraced the opportunity, Evelyn continued to work hard in the forge. She was learning so much, mastering the art of tempering steel and melting iron. With each day that passed, she felt that her skills were improving.

Under Zoey's tutelage, her knowledge of the forge's tools and techniques had grown exponentially. She had learnt how to properly treat metals, how to shape them into a neat finish, and how to make sturdy, elegant clasps for necklace and bracelet chains. Zoey had worked tirelessly alongside her, never leaving her alone to figure something out, and always offering kind words of encouragement.

Each working morning, Evelyn looked forward to entering the forge, enthusiastic in the knowledge that she would be able to practice her skills, continuing to learn and improve. Though her journey as a jeweller had only just begun, she already felt more capable and confident. Not only was she learning a trade, but she was also in a position to contribute to the household.

Having got the hang of the fundamentals, and now able to work alone, sometimes Evelyn would find her mind wandering towards thoughts of the mob who had killed her family. It terrified her to imagine that one day they could catch up with her. So far, nothing had happened to suggest that her worries were justified, but she refused to disregard the notion completely.

As the sun began to set, Evelyn could feel the weight of the day's work settling in her bones. With a sheen of sweat covering her entire body, she wiped her arm over her forehead, appreciative of the momentary sensory relief. It was time for her to go back to the house. As a pleasant wind flowed in through the forge from outside, she quietly tidied up. Feeling content and proud of the work she had done, she carefully put her tools in their proper places, taking a moment to marvel at their intricate beauty, and appreciating the craftsmanship that had gone into each one.

Upon arriving home, she stepped onto the newly-placed fur rug. It had come from a wolf that had attacked Bosun. The defeated animal's meat and bones were used for food and tools, and its pelt was made into the cosy floor covering. Bosun had managed to make it out with only a few scratches and bites, which Evelyn had quickly healed. Since Zoey's acceptance of her, even though she kept her identity concealed from everyone else, Evelyn had been taking steps to embrace her true self – it especially delighted her to do so in instances where she could use her magic to help her new family.

With Bosun having spent the day with Zoey in the shop, the house was empty. Evelyn knew they would be hungry for dinner upon their return home. She was excited at the thought of cooking a delicious meal for them; she had done it many times before, but still enjoyed seeing the smile that crossed Zoey's face in each instance.

Evelyn stepped down into the cellar, feeling the chill in the air as she descended. There was a pheasant that had been caught yesterday and it was still fresh. She chose her ingredients diligently and returned to the kitchen upstairs.

She carefully diced the garlic and parsley. She was more than used to the feel of a knife in her hand, the way it glided through the ingredients so quickly and easily. As she rubbed the seasonings together, they danced in her hands, releasing their aromas into the air around her. When she sprinkled them over the meat before her, it was like a little orchestra of the senses, of which she was the conductor.

She smiled to herself as she added a small amount of goose fat and put the finishing touches to her masterpiece. When she was done, she stepped back and admired her work, basking in the pride that swelled within her. Years of practice had taught her how to deftly work the flavours through the food, thanks to all she had learnt from her mother.

Every time she thought of her parents, a deep

sadness welled up inside. Something as simple as the memory of her mother's laugh – or of her father's strong embrace – was often enough to bring a powerful wave of overbearing nostalgia crashing over her. At times when the grief felt like it was all too much, instead of giving in to the sorrow, Evelyn told herself to embrace Zoey's wise words: "Remember the love, not the loss."

Zoey had taught her to focus on the happy memories and to take comfort in knowing that her family had sacrificed everything so that she could live a life of joy. Self-loathing was no longer an option, and Evelyn found peace in that.

With her meal preparations complete, she lit the fire beneath the wood stove. She knew the meat would take some time to cook, so she decided to have a quick wash. She went to the mirror, soaked a rag with water, and wiped her face clean. Once she had finished, she used the still-damp cloth to soothe her arms, noticing the bruises and scrapes that showed evidence of her labour in the forge. Predominantly though, despite the amount of time that had passed since she'd been chased from her hometown, the scars from the fierce hound that bit her were still visible.

The delicate candlelight dancing behind her filled the room with a warm, golden glow. As she stared at her reflection, Evelyn traced her fingers along the curves and shadows of her face. She looked tired, but strong; there was a glint of something indefinable yet unmistakably powerful in her gaze. Taking a deep breath, she smiled at the mirror and spoke aloud with pride, her voice firm and unshakeable.

"I am a good person. Being a witch doesn't make me bad. It doesn't make me evil. I am who I am, and I'm trying my best."

"I couldn't agree more," said a voice from behind her.

When Evelyn spun around and saw that Zoey was observing her, her cheeks flushed a deep crimson colour. She hadn't been aware that her girlfriend had returned home.

Raising her hand in a cheerful greeting, Zoey let out a lighthearted chuckle and beamed a beautiful smile from ear to ear as she sweetly brushed a lock of hair out of her face.

"Sorry to startle you," she said. "I was going to leave you to it, but upon overhearing what you were saying, I couldn't help but comment."

"That's ok," said Evelyn.

With a heart full of affection, Evelyn approached Zoey with gentle steps. Closing the distance between them, when their eyes met, she couldn't help but mirror the infectious joy on her girlfriend's face. Evelyn then wrapped her arms around Zoey, pulling her into a tender embrace.

"I'm so grateful that you've set up the stove," said Zoey. "We'll be able to have a wonderful meal tonight. First though, there's something I'd like to give you before we eat."

Pleasantly surprised, Evelyn stepped back with a smile, slowly nodding her head in agreement. She then stooped to stroke Bosun's fur as he ran joyfully towards her in greeting.

Evelyn wandered into their bedroom with great interest. Perching herself on the edge of the mattress and waiting for Zoey to arrive, she felt a strange sense of anticipation, as if something magical was about to happen. She glanced around the room, her gaze settling on a crack in the wall. She didn't know what to expect, but was looking forward to finding out what Zoey had in store for her.

Zoey approached Evelyn and placed a delicate ornate box into her hands. It was small and didn't weigh much.

Evelyn smiled in appreciation as she opened the little box, her breath catching when she saw what was inside. She reached in and slowly removed a delicate silver bracelet chain with a metal heart charm dangling from it. In the centre of the heart was a deep red ruby that gleamed brightly in the light. Feeling overcome with emotion, Evelyn clenched the precious trinket and held it close to her chest. Tears began to well in her eyes.

"Thank you," she said. "It's beautiful. I'm touched."

Delighted that the present had brought such satisfaction, Zoey giggled softly as she gazed affectionately at Evelyn.

"I'm so proud of you, Evelyn. You've finally learnt to accept and appreciate yourself. I felt that I wanted to do more than just say it with words though, hence the little something from me to you."

Zoey bent forward, and Evelyn hugged her tightly in a gesture of warmth and adoration.

"I love you, Evelyn."

"I love you, Zoey."

The pair settled onto the bed, appreciating the comfort of the soft mattress and the floral-scented pillows. As they lay intertwined in each other's arms, Evelyn couldn't help but feel an overwhelming sense of gratitude towards Zoey – not only had Zoey done so much for her, but she had such a beautiful soul. With Zoey's unwavering support and encouragement, Evelyn had finally started to see that she was worthy; no longer did she feel uncomfortable and ashamed of the taboo nature of her powers, or of the fact that she was a witch.

In that tender moment, as Evelyn gazed into Zoey's eyes, a profound certainty settled within her heart. It was a knowing, an understanding that she had found something extraordinary. When Zoey's lips met hers for a gentle kiss, Evelyn felt the echoes of a healing embrace, a symbol of closure to the wounds of the past. With that sweet connection, she recognised that it was time to release the grip of history and embrace the unwritten pages of the future, for they would face it together, in strength and in solidarity.